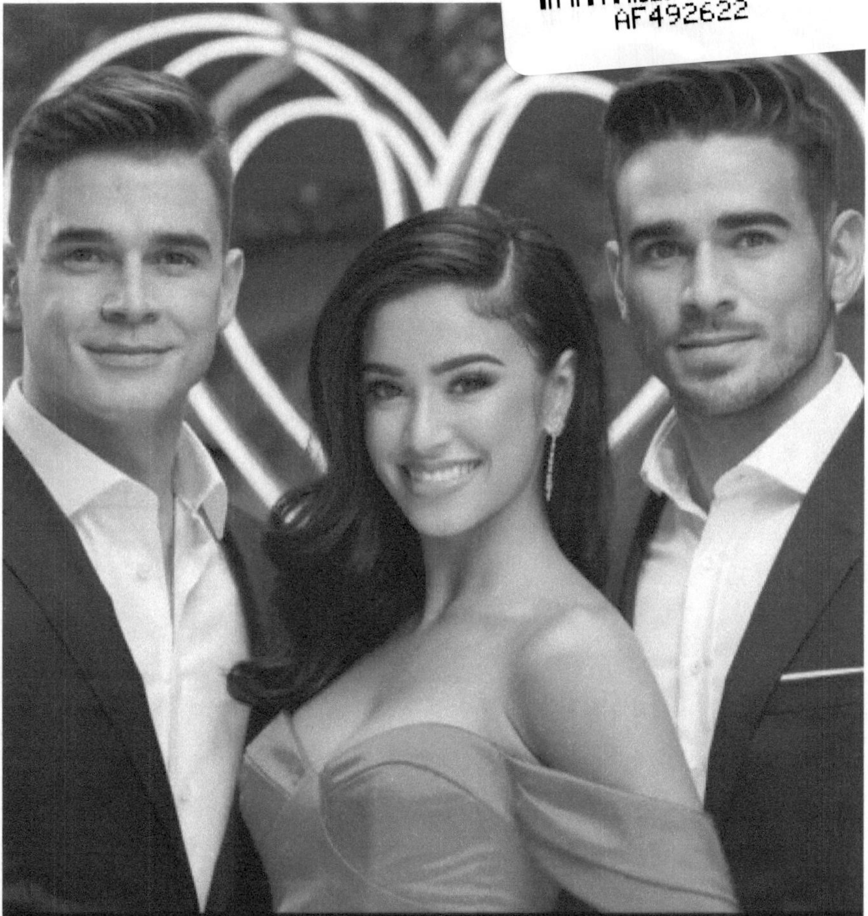

DUALITY

NADEERA GOONETILLEKE

THE WEIGHT OF CHOICE

Duality

Nadeera Goonetilleke

Published by Nadeera Goonetilleke, 2024.

COPYRIGHT PAGE

Title: Duality
Subtitle: The Weight of Choice
By Nadeera Goonetilleke

Copyright © 2004 Nadeera Goonetilleke

All rights reserved. No part of this book may be reproduced, stored in a retrieval system, or transmitted in any form or by any means—electronic, mechanical, photocopying, recording, or otherwise—without the prior written permission of the author, except in the case of brief quotations in reviews or articles.

Disclaimer: This book is a work of fiction. Names, characters, places, and incidents are products of the author's imagination or used fictitiously. Any resemblance to actual events, locales, or persons, living or dead, is entirely coincidental.

While every precaution has been taken in the preparation of this book, the publisher assumes no responsibility for errors or omissions, or for damages resulting from the use of the information contained herein.

DUALITY

First edition. November 5, 2024.

Copyright © 2024 Nadeera Goonetilleke.

ISBN: 979-8227984883

Written by Nadeera Goonetilleke.

TABLE OF CONTENTS

Chapter 1: A World of Her Own

Chapter 1:
A World of Her Own

Liana had spent the last two years at Bliss & Beauty, weaving herself into the fabric of the salon like an artist adding color to a canvas. With a flair for style and an eye for detail, she had become a beloved figure, transforming every haircut into a mini-revolution. Her clients weren't just customers; they were friends who trusted her with their hair—and their stories. For them, a visit to Liana was more than a routine appointment; it was an experience that left them feeling valued and understood.

The salon pulsed with life each day, the familiar hum of hair dryers blending with soft chatter and laughter. It was a place where young professionals mingled with socialites, all drawn in by the promise of luxury. Most of the Clients often arrived early, eagerly waiting for Liana to become available, knowing that her capable hands would craft more than just a style; she would create a moment of joy and rejuvenation.

There was an undeniable warmth about her. Liana greeted everyone with a smile that could brighten even the cloudiest day. Her bright eyes sparkled with genuine interest as she listened to their tales—of worries, triumphs, and everything in between. She had a gift for making her clients feel like they were the only person in the room, that their experiences mattered, and that they were worthy of indulgence.

On one particular Thursday morning, the sun poured through the salon windows, casting a golden glow on the buzzing space. Regular clients gathered in the waiting area, stealing glances at Liana as she meticulously arranged her tools—brushes and scissors gleaming under the soft salon lights.

A middle-aged gentleman approached her, a hint of uncertainty in his eyes. "Excuse me, do you know if you have a booking for some one? I didn't make an appointment."

Liana's smile widened, radiating warmth. "Well, sir, I do have an appointment in about half an hour. But I can certainly fit you in until then."

As she settled him into the chair, her movements were graceful, as if she were dancing to an unspoken rhythm. Known for her ability to create styles that reflected her clients' personalities, it was as if Liana could see into their souls and breathe life into their dreams with every snip and stroke.

After the haircut, the man beamed at his reflection. "Girl, I swear, my hair hasn't looked this good in years! Thank you! My wife is going to be so surprised—ha ha!" He slipped a fifty-dollar note into her hand as a tip, his gratitude genuine.

"You're too kind!" she replied, touched. "Honestly, it's my clients who make this job so enjoyable. I wouldn't be here without you all." He patted her shoulder, and with a cheerful goodbye, he was off, leaving her feeling light-hearted.

As Liana worked, the stories of her clients flowed around her like a comforting blanket—each narrative a piece of the intricate mosaic of their lives. Over the years, she had become a confidante, a kind-hearted presence who listened without judgment. Whether it was family drama, job stress, or romantic troubles, each appointment brought a new tale, a new insight into the human experience.

Yet, outside the vibrant world of the salon, Liana's life was quieter. She was a convent girl, having lost her parents in a tragic car accident. Her uncle had taken her in, ensuring her education in a convent hostel, where she first discovered her love for hairstyling by cutting the hair of her fellow students. Those memories tugged at her heart, bittersweet but cherished. Now, she lived in a small apartment in the city.

While her days were filled with the salon's energy, her evenings passed in serene solitude. She found peace in coming home to a quiet space, often curling up with a good book or experimenting with new styling techniques. But beneath her composed exterior lay a yearning—a small but persistent desire for something more—a spark, a connection, a reminder that her own story was waiting to unfold.

As the last appointment wrapped up, Liana lingered for a moment, watching the sun dip below the horizon. Once the last employee had left, she locked the door behind her, handing over the key to the security guard. With a contented sigh, she stepped into the night, ready to embrace whatever came next.

Chapter 2:
A New Face in the Salon

Morning sunlight streamed through the wide windows of *Bliss & Beauty*, casting a warm glow over the salon as Liana settled in for her day. Although she had arrived a few minutes late, the usual hum of activity filled the air, and no one seemed to mind. The team was already at work, and the sounds of hairdryers, laughter, and greetings mingled with soft background music.

At the front desk, Madam Jean, the salon owner, waited with arms crossed and a gentle smile.

"Good morning, Madam!" Liana greeted, a hint of apology in her voice.

"Good morning, dear! Just wanted to catch you before I head out for the day. I'll be out of town until next week, so I'm counting on you to close up as usual. Remember to hand the keys to security, and give me a call if anything comes up."

"Of course, Madam. Safe travels—I'll take care of everything here."

With a nod, Madam Jean turned and headed for the door, her heels clicking softly against the floor as she left. Liana exhaled, relieved. Since starting here, she had grown close to Madam Jean, viewing her almost as a mentor. After her years at the convent, the salon felt like a second home, and Madam Jean's gentle support had made that possible.

The morning was slow. After making herself a coffee, Liana took a moment to arrange her tools, savoring the quiet as she hummed a tune. She glanced around the space, reflecting on how different her life was now compared to her childhood in the convent, where her uncle had placed her after her parents passed away. Though her uncle provided for her education and needs, life at the convent had taught her resilience, patience, and self-reliance.

Lost in thought, she was jolted back to the present by the sudden clatter of the salon door being flung open. A young man, likely not much older than twenty-five, stepped inside, his confident stride and slightly disheveled hair immediately drawing attention.

At the reception desk, Lily greeted him cheerfully. "Good morning! How can I help you?"

"I'm here for the first time, looking for the best haircut around," he replied with a grin, clearly amused.

"Oh, you've come to the right place," Lily chuckled, directing him toward Liana.

As he approached, Liana met his gaze, sensing a quiet self-assuredness in him.

"Good morning," he said, flashing a charming smile. "I'm Christy."

"Nice to meet you. So, what can I do for you?" Liana asked.

"I'm a bit particular," he said, settling into the chair as she draped a cape around him. "I like a clean, polished look... but with some personality. Nothing too conservative."

She nodded, her professional instincts kicking in as she took in the contours of his face, the texture of his hair, and his overall style. "Got it. A clean cut with some flair to give it a modern touch. I'll add texture on top to keep it versatile while keeping the sides sharp."

"Oh... sounds like you already know exactly what I want," he remarked, watching her in the mirror, a slight smile playing at his lips.

"It's part of the job. The challenge makes it fun," she replied with a small smile as she started combing through his hair.

As her hands moved with practiced ease, she felt Christy's gaze on her, as though he was studying her just as much as she was analyzing his hair.

"So, how'd you end up here?" he asked, breaking the silence.

She paused for a moment, reflecting. "It's been a journey. I grew up in a convent after losing my parents. My uncle supported me, and after I graduated, I trained in beauty and hair styling. The salon felt like the perfect place to combine creativity with my need to connect with people."

"That's... different. I mean, growing up in a convent and now working in a salon—it's like two worlds apart."

"It is. But both taught me a lot—discipline, independence, resilience. And here, I get to help people feel their best, which is a reward in itself."

He nodded thoughtfully, his expression genuine as he listened. There was something about him that felt grounded despite his easygoing demeanor.

"Do most of your clients trust you to work your magic, or do they know exactly what they want?" he asked.

"A bit of both," she replied, smiling as she snipped carefully around his face. "I have regulars who leave it all to me, and others, like you, who come in with a vision. I enjoy both—it keeps things interesting."

He laughed, a warm sound that seemed to relax her further. "I suppose I am a little particular. But I like the idea of a haircut that's... unique to me."

She took a step back, examining her work before giving a few final touches. Satisfied, she met his gaze in the mirror. He looked at his reflection, running a hand through his hair, a pleased grin spreading across his face.

"This is perfect," he said, turning to her directly. "It's exactly what I had in mind. Thank you."

"Glad you're happy with it," she replied, a sense of pride warming her chest. "That's what I aim for."

As he rose from the chair, their eyes met in the mirror, a brief, intimate exchange that felt almost personal.

"I'll be back," he said, handing her a fifty-dollar bill, his tone soft but confident, as though it were a promise.

With a final smile, he paid the cashier and left the salon, his presence somehow lingering even after the door closed behind him. She took a breath, feeling a surprising thrill. It wasn't often a new client left such an impression, and she couldn't help but wonder if Christy's promise to return was just a polite comment—or if, perhaps, she might indeed be seeing him again soon.

Chapter 3:
A Whirlwind of Emotions

As Liana stirred the pot of simmering pasta, the delightful aroma filled her cozy apartment. The gentle sound of boiling water mixed with the soft hum of her favorite playlist, creating the perfect ambiance for a peaceful evening. Yet, as she cooked, her mind kept drifting back to Christy and their lighthearted conversation at the salon.

His easygoing nature and warm smile had left an impression on her, unlike any other client. Sure, she often received admiring glances from clients who appreciated her skills, but Christy was different. His jovial spirit and genuine curiosity about her life made her feel at ease, like they were old friends catching up rather than a stylist and a client. She chuckled to herself, wondering if she was developing a silly crush on him.

What would it be like if someone like Christy expressed romantic interest? She mused. Would she be bold enough to act on it, or would her insecurities pull her back into her shell?

Shaking her head, she tried to dismiss the flutter of feelings brewing in her stomach. This must be just a fleeting crush, she reassured herself. After all, it had been ages since she'd felt anything resembling attraction. Yet, the thought of seeing him again ignited a spark of hope in her heart.

But weeks turned into months, and despite her anticipation, Christy's absence weighed on her. Each day, she wondered if he would return, but life at the salon continued in its usual rhythm, filled with clients and gossip. Liana focused on her work, reminding herself that it was for the best.

One evening, as the sun dipped below the horizon, casting a warm glow in the salon, the door swung open, and a familiar face rushed in, breaking her reverie.

"Hi, Miss... By the way, I never got your name!" Christy exclaimed, his hair tousled and his expression animated.

"I'm Liana!" she replied, unable to suppress a smile at the sight of him.

"Liana! Such a beautiful name," he said with a grin, his eyes gleaming with excitement. "I'm in a bit of a bind—I need a quick haircut! Tomorrow's my sister's wedding, and with all the duties that come with being the only son and brother, I'm feeling a little overwhelmed!"

Liana couldn't help but chuckle at his flustered demeanor. "You're just in time! We're about to close in half an hour, but I can fit you in if you don't mind waiting."

"Not at all!" He plopped himself down on a waiting chair, grabbing a magazine and flipping through the pages with casual ease.

As Liana finished with her current client, she felt a mix of excitement and nerves. What hairstyle would suit him best? She contemplated, trying to suppress her eagerness. Once her client left, she turned to Christy. "Alright, let's get you looking dapper! What are you thinking for your sister's big day?"

"I'm a bit particular," he admitted, a playful glint in his eyes. "But I trust you, Liana. Surprise me!"

"Challenge accepted!" she laughed, grabbing her scissors and comb. As she worked, she couldn't help but steal glances at him in the mirror. His easy smile and charming demeanor made her heart flutter, and the playful banter flowed naturally between them.

"So, what's your sister like?" she asked, snipping away, letting her creativity flourish.

"Oh, she's a whirlwind of energy—always organizing everything! I'm just the backup dancer in her show," he joked. "But she deserves all the attention tomorrow."

"I'm sure she'll be thrilled to see you all spruced up. What about you? Do you have a dance prepared?" Liana teased, trying to keep the mood light.

"Only the classic 'two left feet' routine! But I'll make it work," he laughed, leaning back as she shaped his hair.

Time slipped away as they chatted, and Liana lost herself in the rhythm of snipping and styling, feeling a sense of connection that was hard to ignore. Before she knew it, the clock read nearly 7 PM, and she stepped back to admire her handiwork.

"Wow, Liana! This is fantastic!" Christy exclaimed, inspecting his new look in the mirror. His hair was styled perfectly—clean and polished, with just the right amount of flair to show off his personality.

"Glad you like it!" she replied, feeling a swell of pride. "It's always fun to add a little creativity into the mix."

As he turned to face her, his expression shifted slightly, and for a moment, the air around them seemed to thicken with unspoken words. "I'm really sorry for keeping you so late. Let me give you a ride home," he offered, a hint of concern lacing his tone.

Liana hesitated for a moment, a mixture of excitement and reluctance battling within her. A ride home with Christy? But she knew she should be careful not to read too much into it.

"Are you sure? I don't want to impose," she replied, her heart racing.

"Not at all! I insist. Besides, it's the least I can do after you worked your magic on my hair," he said, his confidence radiating.

With a small smile and a nod, Liana agreed. As they walked to his car, the evening air felt electric with possibility, and for the first time in a long while, Liana allowed herself to feel a flicker of hope. Maybe there was more to this connection than she had initially thought, and perhaps, just maybe, she was ready to explore it.

Chapter 4:
Unexpected Sparks

As Liana waited by the car, she saw Christy walking over with an easy smile. Reaching her side, he opened the door with a graceful bow and extended his hand in invitation, his eyes dancing with a playful glint. Liana felt an unexpected warmth in her cheeks as she thanked him and slipped into the car, trying to ignore the flutter of nerves that wasn't typically her style. Usually, she was the one who confidently chatted with clients, holding her own without a hint of bashfulness, but something about this moment felt different.

As they settled into the drive, she broke the silence, hoping casual conversation would ease her jittery nerves. "So, your sister's getting married tomorrow...is it a love marriage?"

"Absolutely! She met her university Romeo," he chuckled, glancing over with a fond smile. "They were in the same engineering faculty and somehow, through exams and projects, they ended up here—at the altar."

"Lucky people..." Liana murmured, the words slipping out before she realized it.

Christy gave her a curious look, catching the wistful tone. "And what about you? No Romeo in your life?"

Liana's lips curved in a thoughtful smile as she met his gaze. "Let's just say I like to wait on things, let them take their time." Sensing that she didn't want to linger on that topic, she smoothly steered the conversation elsewhere. "So, are you working?"

He nodded, a bright smile spreading across his face. "Yep, I work in advertising. I handle both the marketing and creative sides, so I'm constantly on the move—meeting clients and setting up campaigns. I also help manage my dad's hotel, so there's hardly a moment to catch my breath... or even get a haircut, it seems!" He chuckled, adding a lighthearted touch to his busy schedule.

Liana laughed with him, shaking her head. "Sounds like busy doesn't even begin to cover it."

"Would you mind if I asked for your number? That way, I can make appointments ahead of time instead of showing up last minute."

Without hesitation, Liana handed over her number. A moment later, her phone rang, and she saw Christy's number light up her screen, making her smile—now she had his number too.

They arrived at her apartment complex all too quickly, and as she unbuckled her seatbelt, she turned to him with a warm smile. "Would you like to come up for coffee?"

Christy shook his head with an apologetic smile. "Thanks, but I'm swamped with last-minute wedding duties. Of course, no worries. She stepped out, but before she could head inside, he called out to her.

"Liana," he said, leaning out of the window with a grin, "I'll bring some cakes for you and the salon team after the wedding—not tomorrow, but the day after."

"That's kind of you, Christy. I'm sure everyone would love that." She waved, watching him drive off with a small smile, feeling a lightness she couldn't quite explain.

Chapter 5:
A Sweet Surprise

It was early afternoon at Bliss & Beauty, and the team was just finishing up a lively morning rush when Christy strolled in, arms filled with what looked like a bakery's entire stock. The sweet aroma of freshly baked cakes wafted through the salon, drawing every eye in his direction. Christy handed a large box to Liana with a warm smile.

"I might have gone a bit overboard," he chuckled. "There's plenty in here for the whole team—and a little extra for you to enjoy later."

Liana laughed, taking the box and glancing at the team, who were all staring, wide-eyed and more than a little curious. "Thanks, Christy. This will definitely be a hit."

As soon as he left, the salon exploded with chatter. Emma, one of the stylists, leaned over the counter with a mischievous grin. "So... Liana, care to explain why Mr. Handsome over there brought you half a bakery?"

Liana rolled her eyes, trying not to blush. "Oh, please. He just wanted to thank us for the haircut."

Emma raised an eyebrow. "Uh-huh. Clients always bring wedding cake leftovers for us. Totally normal."

Kelly, another stylist, giggled as she reached for a slice. "I mean, come on, Liana, he looked like he was here for more than just the haircut."

Liana shrugged, trying to keep it casual. "Well, his sister just got married yesterday.

"Hmm..." Emma mused with a playful wink. "Family man, generous.

The team burst out laughing, and Liana joined in, feeling a strange thrill she hadn't quite experienced before.

Later that evening, as she was unwinding at home, her phone buzzed unexpectedly. Glancing down, she saw Christy's name light up the screen. Her heart skipped a beat.

"Hello?" she answered, trying to keep her voice steady.

"Hey, Liana! It's Christy," he replied, his voice warm and cheerful. "I just wanted to check if the cakes were enough for everyone—and if they were any good. Did the team enjoy them?"

Liana smiled, relaxing a little. "More than enough, and they were a huge hit. I barely escaped all the questions they had about you."

He laughed. "Questions, huh? Am I that mysterious?"

"Well, let's just say you left a bit of an impression," she teased, trying to keep her tone light.

They chatted about the wedding—Liana learned all about his sister's big day, from the flowers to the mishap with the DJ who played the wrong song during the first dance. Christy's relaxed tone and the way he joked about the day's little disasters put her completely at ease, as if they'd known each other far longer than they had.

"Speaking of relaxing," he said after a pause, "how about a coffee on Sunday? I know it's last minute, but... well, it'd be nice to catch up, no wedding stress involved."

Her heart fluttered. Coffee? A one-on-one meeting wasn't something she was used to, and her convent upbringing made her a little hesitant. But there was something so friendly and genuine in his invitation that she found herself nodding.

"Alright," she said finally. "Sunday sounds great."

Chapter 6:
At the Canvas Café

The Canvas Café was tucked away in a quiet corner of the bustling city, famous for its cozy ambiance and the scent of freshly brewed coffee mingling with warm pastries. Inside, the walls were decorated with local artwork, paintings of vivid landscapes, and abstract designs that matched the café's name. Soft indie music floated in the background, and warm, dim lighting cast a golden glow over the rustic wooden tables, creating an intimate, relaxed atmosphere.

Liana arrived a bit early, admiring the café's charming vibe as she waited for Christy. Her thoughts wandered, nerves and curiosity intertwining. Just then, the door swung open, and Christy walked in, spotting her instantly. With a wide grin, he made his way to her table.

"Wow, this place is even cozier than I imagined," he said, pulling a small gift-wrapped package from behind his back, extending it to her. "A little something, since I kept you waiting."

She blinked, surprised. "For me? I wasn't waiting that long."

"Consider it a thank-you for the patience you showed during my frantic haircut emergency," he chuckled, taking a seat across from her.

Unwrapping it, she found a small, framed painting of a sunset by the sea. It was beautiful, simple, yet captivating. "This is lovely, Christy," she said, touched.

"Thought it might remind you of relaxing moments... since we both could use more of those," he replied with a wink. She couldn't help but smile, his playful charm already disarming her usual guarded demeanor.

As they chatted, she noticed his cologne—a warm, woody scent with a hint of spice. It was subtle but had a way of lingering, making her pulse quicken every time he leaned a little closer.

""Christy, you mentioned your advertising work. What's the most exciting project you've been involved in lately?" Liana asked, leaning forward with genuine curiosity as she took another sip of her coffee.

He grinned, the spark in his eyes indicating he was eager to share. "Oh, there are so many! Recently, I worked on a campaign for a new line of eco-friendly products. It was all about creativity and sustainability, which is something I'm really passionate about."

"That sounds amazing!" Liana exclaimed, her interest piqued. "What was your role in the campaign?"

"I was involved in everything from brainstorming ideas to executing the visuals," he said, animatedly. "We created some really eye-catching ads that incorporated nature and vibrant colors. I even got to lead a photo-shoot in a beautiful garden."

"Wow that must have been a dream come true!" Liana said, her eyes wide with excitement. "Did you have a favorite part of the project?"

"Definitely the photo-shoot," he replied, his enthusiasm infectious. "Working with the team and seeing the ideas come to life was incredible. Plus, the models we used were so much fun to collaborate with."

Liana chuckled, imagining the lively atmosphere. "I can just picture it. Do you ever get to be in front of the camera, or are you always behind the scenes?"

"Mostly behind the scenes," he admitted, a playful smirk on his face. "But I did end up in one of the ads for a client once. They needed a last-minute model, and I thought, why not? It was both nerve-wracking and hilarious!"

"I would love to see that ad," she laughed. "You'll have to show it to me sometime. You're quite the multifaceted talent, aren't you?"

Christy leaned in slightly, a playful grin spreading across his face. "Thanks, Liana. I really appreciate that. It's not just about the work; it's about the stories we create and the connections we make along the way." He paused, his gaze locking onto hers. "And speaking of connections, I've always felt that the best campaigns are the ones that resonate on a personal level. Like what you're doing here at the salon—it's not just about hair; it's about making people feel beautiful and confident."

Liana felt her heart flutter at his words, the sincerity in his voice captivating her. She realized she was hanging on every syllable, lost in the warmth of his presence. "I never thought about it that way," she replied, her voice slightly breathless. "You're right; it's about the impact we have on people's lives."

Christy noticed the way her eyes sparkled with admiration, a soft blush creeping onto her cheeks. "Looks like I've spellbound you with my marketing wisdom," he teased lightly, a knowing smile dancing on his lips. "But really, it's the passion behind what we do that makes the difference. I see that same passion in you, Liana. It's inspiring."

Liana smiled, a mix of embarrassment and delight flooding her. "I guess I just never realized how intertwined our worlds can be," she admitted, feeling a warmth spread through her. "You make it sound so enchanting."

His gaze softened, and for a moment, the lively café faded away, leaving just the two of them in their shared moment of connection. "Well, Liana, you're a part of that enchantment too," Christy said, his voice low and sincere. "Never underestimate the magic you bring to your craft."

Liana felt her breath catch, the weight of his words lingering in the air between them.

Without warning, he reached across the table and gently squeezed her hand, catching her off-guard. The warmth of his hand, combined with that intoxicating cologne, made her lean slightly closer, almost as if he were pulling her in like a magnet.

"You alright?" he asked, noticing her shift and holding her gaze with a slight smirk.

"Just... wasn't expecting that," she stammered, a blush creeping up her cheeks.

"Good," he said softly, leaning in closer. "Sometimes, the best moments are the ones you don't see coming."

The intensity in his gaze made her heart flutter, and for a moment, they sat in comfortable silence, each lost in thought.

Finally, she broke the spell with a playful question. "So, tell me, with all this 'living in the moment' stuff... what does a guy like you do for fun?"

"Oh, you mean besides last-minute haircuts and showing up unannounced with wedding cake?" he laughed, squeezing her hand once more. "Well, I travel a lot, love a good spontaneous road trip. And I suppose I have this habit of turning even the most serious situations into a joke."

"Ah, I see," she replied with a smirk, her heart racing at his touch. "So, you're the guy who can make any moment feel like an adventure?"

"Something like that," he said, laughing softly. "And, maybe... convince a reserved salon owner to grab coffee with me on a Sunday?"

She blushed, but a laugh escaped her lips. "Alright, maybe you've got a point there."

As they continued their conversation, each playful quip seemed to pull them closer, and with every glance, touch, and laugh, Liana felt her usual caution melting away in his presence.

Chapter 7:
A Trim, a Tug, and a Twist of Fate

After a quick lunch in the pantry the following afternoon, Liana returned to the salon, a soft smile lingering on her lips as she recalled her time with Christy. Stepping inside, she noticed a young man with a lively little girl in the waiting area. The girl was bouncing on the edge of her seat, her bright energy practically lighting up the room as she wriggled and fidgeted with boundless excitement.

The little girl swung her legs and giggled as her caregiver tried everything to keep her in one place. Liana strolled over, intrigued by the lively pair.

"Hello there! May I help you with something?" she asked warmly.

The man looked up with a relieved smile. "Yes, please! I'm David, and this little mischief could really use a trim. She's not exactly the easiest client—do you think you can handle her?"

Liana smiled warmly, keeping her tone light yet reassuring. "Absolutely, David. We're well-equipped for energetic clients here. I'll make sure she's comfortable, and we'll keep it fun for her. Let's get started, shall we?"

Liana chuckled, kneeling down to the girl's level. "Your little one is full of energy!"

David grinned, shaking his head. "No, she's actually my sister's daughter, but with the way she keeps me on my toes, I'm starting to feel like her full-time babysitter!"

The little girl tugged on David's sleeve, chattering away about her favorite toys, her wide eyes darting around the salon, eager to explore.

"Alright," Liana said with a determined grin, standing up. "Let's see if we can tackle this challenge together, shall we?"

The task felt more like a wrestling match than a haircut. Liana gently held the girl's head still while David distracted her with funny faces and whispered promises of candy if she cooperated. Every so often, Liana and David's hands brushed as they worked to keep the little one steady, and she found herself glancing at him, caught off guard by a small but undeniable warmth at their shared effort.

At one point, Liana felt—and she was sure David felt it too—that they were both exhausted parents on duty.

As they finally managed to finish the trim, David leaned back with a sigh, clearly relieved. "Wow that was more of a workout than I anticipated!"

Liana laughed, brushing stray hairs off her shirt. "Tell me about it. But hey, mission accomplished!"

David reached into his pocket, pulling out his business card along with a generous tip. "Thank you, you're a lifesaver. I owe you one."

"All in a day's work," she replied with a grin, pocketing the card. "But honestly, it was a pleasure. You're great with kids."

David shrugged modestly. "I really enjoy spending time with kids. I'll be back next Saturday to finally get my own hair sorted out—hopefully without the chaos this time. Are you available in the morning?"

"Absolutely! I'd love to see you again, and I promise it'll be a much calmer experience. Just let me know what time works for you!"

David nodded, a hint of uncertainty in his eyes. "I can't promise an exact time since my schedule can be a bit unpredictable, but I'll definitely try to make it Saturday morning.

Liana smiled understandingly. "No problem, David!

"See you then!" he said, waving as he headed out the door. Liana watched him go, a flutter of excitement stirring in her chest as she realized that her day had taken an unexpectedly delightful turn.

Chapter 8:
The Early Bird

Emma, as always, was the first to arrive at the salon, dropped off by her husband on his way to the office. She settled in, organized her workspace, and enjoyed her breakfast, savoring the quiet before the day began. When she heard the door chime, she turned with a smile, assuming it was the receptionist.

But it wasn't.

"Good morning, sir," Emma greeted warmly, a bit surprised to see a client this early. "Do you have an appointment, and who's your stylist?"

"Oh, I didn't specify an exact time, but I mentioned that I would come in on Saturday morning."

Emma nodded with understanding. "Well, give me just a few minutes, and I'll set you up."

"Thanks," he said, glancing around. "But actually, I was hoping to have my hair done by... what's her name... tall, slim...?"

"Liana!" Emma exclaimed with a knowing smile. "She'll be here any moment. Feel free to take a seat in the meantime," she said, handing him a newspaper.

"Thanks, very kind of you," he replied, settling into a seat and flipping through the pages.

About thirty minutes later, Liana entered the salon, blissfully unaware of a client waiting for her. She headed straight for the pantry, poured herself her usual coffee, and took a moment to savor it, preparing herself for the day ahead. Emma sauntered over with a playful grin.

"Liana, your early bird is here!" Emma called out, pointing to the seating area. "He's been waiting for you since the crack of dawn!"

Liana raised an eyebrow and set her coffee down with a soft sigh. "Okay, thanks, Emma. I'll be ready in a couple of minutes," she replied, preparing to dive into her work.

"Good morning, sir," she greeted with a professional smile as she approached the client, who was still buried in the newspaper. "I'm Liana—may I help you?"

The gentleman set down the newspaper and glanced up, and Liana's smile froze, her eyes widening slightly.

It was David.

A flicker of recognition danced across his face, and he returned her surprise with an easy smile. "Well, good morning, Liana. Nice to see you again."

Liana quickly composed herself, a faint blush creeping up her cheeks. "David! I didn't expect you so early... actually!"

He chuckled. "I thought I'd be your first customer today. Figured I'd save myself from the lunchtime rush."

"Good thinking," Liana said, allowing her initial surprise to melt into a warm smile. She gestured toward the chair and asked, "How can I assist you today?"

David settled in, his eyes crinkling with a hint of playfulness. "Just a trim. But hey, if you feel inspired, I'll leave the creativity up to you."

Liana grinned, combing through his hair. "Brave of you, David. But don't worry—I'll keep it professional."

He laughed softly. "I trust you. After all, I've seen you handle more challenging clients," he teased, referring to the little girl they'd managed the previous day.

She chuckled, remembering the challenge. "Oh, absolutely! That was quite the workout. She's fortunate to have such a patient uncle."

I love kids; their antics really help relieve stress." David grinned.

Their playful banter flowed effortlessly as Liana worked, each lighthearted exchange infusing the salon with a warm, inviting atmosphere. It felt more like an easy catch-up between old friends over coffee than a simple haircut. Emma, observing from across the room, couldn't help but smile at the enchanting scene, taking note of the shared glances and laughter that danced between them.

In the midst of their conversation, David looked over to Liana with a warm, appreciative smile. "You know, Liana, I think you've turned me into a true professional. Thank you for all you've done," he said, sincerity filling his tone. "You've done an exceptional job. I'm truly happy with the progress."

Liana, taken aback by his genuine praise, responded with a modest smile. "Thank you, David. That means a lot coming from you."

He hesitated for a moment, then added, "By the way, could I get your card? I'd like to send you an invitation for the award ceremony."

"Oh, what's the occasion?" she asked, her curiosity piqued.

David's eyes sparkled as he replied, "Our company, Techno Bridge Solutions, has just been recognized as the most prestigious IT company in the country."

"That's incredible!" Liana exclaimed, genuinely thrilled for him. "Congratulations, David! That's wonderful news. You must be proud."

"Thank you. It's been quite a journey," he replied, a look of satisfaction shining in his eyes.

Liana reached into her bag and pulled out a new business card. David accepted it, then tilted his head slightly as he studied her. "If you don't mind, could you write down your home address? I think it wouldn't be very polite to send the invitation to the salon just for you."

Without hesitation, Liana flipped the card and carefully noted her address on the back, appreciating the professional touch in his request.

As their conversation drew to a close, David subtly left a generous tip and settled the bill with the cashier, offering her a brief nod of acknowledgment. "Thank you once again, Liana. I'll be in touch. Goodbye for now."

"Goodbye, David. Looking forward to hearing more about the ceremony!"

As soon as he left, Liana searched through her handbag, remembering the card he had given her earlier. "Oh, here it is!" she exclaimed with delight as she pulled it out. To her surprise, she saw that he was the Chairman of Techno Bridge Solutions. An exhilarating thrill coursed through her as she recognized the potential benefits of connecting with someone like him in her career.

Chapter 9:
A Dinner Guest

After a long day, Liana chose to relax with a simple yet comforting meal. She prepared a modest dinner of creamy pasta topped with a light sprinkle of cheese, accompanied by crispy golden chips. Keeping the portions balanced in line with her modest diet, she ensured that each bite would still be satisfying. Once everything was ready, she indulged in a hot shower, allowing the steam to wash away the stress of the day. Feeling rejuvenated, she slipped into a light cotton nightdress, spritzed on a refreshing, lightly scented cologne, and wrapped herself in a cozy housecoat before heading back to the living room.

Just as she switched on the TV and prepared to enjoy her meal, the doorbell rang. *Who could it be at this hour?* She wondered, smiling to herself. *Perhaps it's Doreen, the neighbor,* she thought. Doreen often shared a portion of her grand meals with Liana.

Opening the door with a warm smile, Liana was surprised to find David standing there. "David!" she exclaimed, a bit taken aback.

"Sorry, Liana. I wasn't able to call ahead," he said, rubbing the back of his neck with a hint of sheepishness. "I had a meeting, went home to change, and thought it would be nice to deliver the invitation to you personally.""

"That's absolutely fine! Please, come in," she said, stepping aside to welcome him. David stepped inside, taking in the cozy atmosphere around him. His gaze drifted around the room before he inquired, "Are you staying here alone?"

Liana nodded, smiling. "Yes, it's just me," she said, then briefly shared her story of independence, telling him about her journey and the sense of peace she found in her quiet home.

David listened attentively, nodding with understanding. "It sounds like you've created a wonderful life for yourself, Liana. It's not easy to do what you've done—making a home and a career on your own. That takes strength."

Liana felt a warmth spread through her as she absorbed his words. "By the way," she said, "did you have dinner yet?"

"No, I was planning to eat once I got home," he admitted.

"Well, I'd be happy to share mine! It's nothing fancy, just a modest meal, but I'd enjoy the company," she insisted, hurrying to the kitchen to add a quick salad to the table.

David watched as she set out the simple but appealing spread. The creamy pasta was topped with a light layer of melted cheese, and the chips were perfectly crisped. She had also assembled a fresh salad with greens, tomatoes, and a hint of dressing. The little table was humble, but the care Liana put into arranging it made it feel special.

As they began to eat, David took his first bite, and his face lit up with delight. "Liana, this is fantastic," he said, savoring the delicious blend of flavors. "You really didn't have to go to all this trouble, but I'm so glad you did."

"Thank you," she replied, delighted by his genuine enjoyment.

Between bites, he handed her the invitation, and they talked about the upcoming ceremony. Glancing at the date, Liana's eyes brightened. "It's on the 15th—a Wednesday. I'm off that day, so I can definitely be there."

David smiled, clearly pleased. "I'm looking forward to it. It'll be even better with you there."

As he prepared to leave, Liana felt a deep sense of admiration for David's thoughtful and gracious demeanor. His presence left her feeling appreciated, and as she closed the door behind him, she realized just how much she had grown to admire him. She was left with a sense of warmth that lingered long after he'd gone.

Chapter Title 10:
A Call from the Past

The following morning, as the soft light of dawn filtered through the curtains, Liana stretched and glanced at her phone, still lying on her bedside table. A missed call notification blinked on the screen—Christy. *How did I miss that?* She thought, then remembered her habit of putting her phone on silent mode before bed.

She returned his call just before starting her morning routine. After a few rings, Christy answered. "Hey, Liana! Sorry for calling so late last night. You know how it is—I had a last-minute business trip to Singapore. I got back yesterday evening and I'm off again tomorrow evening. This is the first chance I've had to call and say hello..."

Liana smiled to herself as Christy's voice filled her ear, a constant stream of explanations pouring out with his usual energy. "Christy, it's perfectly alright," she said, trying to break into his chatter. "I assumed you were busy with work. You know how it goes here too—salon life is always a whirlwind."

He chuckled. "I bet it is! But I really want to catch up with you. How about dinner? I know a fantastic restaurant with a top-notch menu. It's super popular with the high society crowd—perfect spot to unwind and have some great food."

For a moment, Liana felt a familiar thrill spark inside her as memories of Christy's captivating charm came rushing back—the way he spoke, his effortless style, and that unforgettable scent of his cologne that lingered in her thoughts even now. She couldn't resist the invitation.

"Alright," she replied, excitement lacing her words. "I'll be ready by 8 p.m."

"Perfect. I'll come to pick you up. See you then," he said warmly. "Take care, Liana."

As she ended the call, a little rush of anticipation filled her morning. She had always admired Christy's charisma and easy charm, and now, she couldn't help but wonder what this evening might bring.

Chapter 11:
Whispers of the Heart

As Liana heard the honk of the car horn, she took one last glance in the mirror. Her purple dress hugged her curves perfectly, her makeup was flawless, and her hair cascaded in soft waves around her shoulders. Satisfied with her appearance, she rushed to the entrance, closing the door behind her and tucking the key into her handbag with a smile.

As she approached the car, Christy stepped out, a charming smile spreading across his face. He opened the door for her and said, "You look absolutely gorgeous tonight."

"Thank you," she replied, blushing slightly as she slid into the seat.

Once they were on the road, Christy reached into his bag and presented her with a beautifully wrapped box. "I picked this up for you from a shop in Singapore," he said, his eyes twinkling with excitement.

Liana hesitated for a moment, remembering how he had offered her a gift on their last outing. "Oh, you really didn't have to," she said, trying to sound casual.

"Come on, take it! I know how much girls love perfumes," he said playfully, nudging the box toward her.

With a reluctant smile, she accepted the gift. "Alright, but only because you insist!"

As they arrived at the restaurant, Liana's breath caught in her throat. The sophistication of the place was breathtaking, with dim lighting and elegant decor that set the mood for an enchanting evening.

Once seated, Christy scanned the high-class menu, pointing out various dishes. "I think you'll love the lobster bisque, and the filet mignon is a must-try," he suggested, his voice smooth and confident.

"Sounds perfect," Liana replied, feeling a thrill at his attention to detail.

Throughout the meal, they engaged in light-hearted banter, their laughter mingling with the soft sounds of the restaurant.

"Hey," Christy said, a playful smile crossing his face, "I've been meaning to ask—what do you think about my culinary skills? How about I cook dinner for you one evening?"

Liana chuckled, a teasing glimmer in her eye. "Sure, as long as you don't set off the smoke alarm!" Christy laughed heartily, his eyes twinkling with amusement. "Oh, come on! I promise I'll keep the fire extinguisher handy.

Liana grinned playfully, "Well, since you're a hotelier, I assume you know all the modern techniques for cooking. You might just surprise me!"

"By the way, I remember you mentioning that you're flying out tomorrow. Is it to Singapore again? When will you be back?" Liana asked.

"Yes, but this time it's not Singapore," Christy replied. "I'm heading to Hong Kong. There are some exciting business opportunities in the advertising field that I want to explore."

"Oh really? What kind of opportunities?" Liana inquired, intrigued.

"Well," Christy began, his voice brightening, "Hong Kong is a vibrant market with a unique blend of East and West. There's a huge demand for creative advertising strategies, especially with brands looking to connect with younger audiences. I'm meeting with a few clients who are interested in digital campaigns and influencer collaborations. It's all about tapping into the local culture while still appealing to global trends. I'm really looking forward to it!"

"That sounds amazing! I can see why you're excited," Liana responded, spellbound by his enthusiasm. "I've heard Hong Kong has such a dynamic atmosphere."

"Absolutely! It's fast-paced, and there's always something happening," Christy said, noticing the spark in her eyes. "Maybe one day you could join me on one of these trips. It would be fun to explore together!"

Liana smiled, her expression playful yet cautious. "Oh, that sounds like a great adventure, Christy! But you know how these business trips can go—sometimes they lead to unexpected opportunities that keep you busy. When do you think you'll be back?"

"I'll be back on Saturday," he replied.

"Saturday, huh? Well, I suppose that gives you a little time to catch your breath before diving back into the hustle," she said lightly. "I hope you'll manage to squeeze in some fun between all those meetings."

"Definitely! I'll make the most of it. Let's catch up when I'm back!"

After they finished their meal, the conversation flowed easily. Liana couldn't help but notice Christy's gaze on her; it was both sexy and romantic, sending butterflies fluttering in her stomach. She struggled to maintain her composure, feeling an unexpected pull toward him.

Christy casually changed the subject, his tone light yet inquisitive. "By the way, are you currently in a relationship with anyone?" he asked, genuinely interested.

Caught off guard, Liana paused for a moment, then leaned in slightly, her eyes sparkling with curiosity. "That's an interesting question! What makes you ask?" she replied, keeping her tone playful and inviting.

Christy smiled, appreciating her cleverness. "I'm just curious, really. I think you're an amazing person, and I'd love to know more about who has the privilege of being in your life," he said, his tone sincere.

Liana smiled thoughtfully, her eyes shining with wisdom. "I tend to take my time when it comes to choosing someone for the future. After all, it's important to find the right fit, don't you think?"

He chuckled softly, but a touch of seriousness began to shadow his expression. "I was just wondering if you might ever consider being my fiancée one day. You know, for marriage."

His words lingered in the air, and Liana's thoughts began to swirl. Memories of David flooded her mind, prompting her to pause. She realized she needed to tread carefully and not rush into any decisions.

"That's quite the proposal," she replied with a playful smile, concealing her inner thoughts. "I believe it's important to take things one step at a time. I want to ensure that I make the best choice for my future."

Christy regarded her with an understanding nod, a flicker of admiration in his eyes. "I appreciate that," he said. "It's good to be thoughtful about these things."

As they continued their conversation, Liana felt a mixture of excitement and caution, unsure of where her heart would lead her next.

After a pleasant evening together, Christy pulled up in front of her apartment and parked. "Here we are," he said with a warm smile, turning to face her. Liana returned the smile, feeling a mix of gratitude and reluctance.

"Thanks for the ride, Christy," she replied, opening the door.

"Anytime! Take care, and I'll see you soon," he said, waving as she stepped out. With one last glance, he drove away, leaving Liana standing on the sidewalk with a sense of warmth from their time together.

After a refreshing shower, Liana slipped into bed, the cool sheets wrapping around her like a comforting embrace. Tomorrow was her day off, and with it came the thrill of the award ceremony. As she lay there, her thoughts began to drift, analyzing every detail of her life. Christy came from a wealthy family, while she had only her job at the beauty salon and her uncle—her mother's brother—who was now old and felt more like a distant memory than a reliable source of support. This disparity weighed heavily on her mind, raising unsettling questions. Would his family genuinely accept someone like her—a girl devoted to her craft and striving to create a life for herself against all odds?

Romantic thoughts twirled in her mind as she recalled the sweet words Christy often whispered. But could she truly trust that his feelings would last? What if, when faced with his family's expectations, he changed his tune? Liana recognized the importance of staying grounded, keeping her heart steady and not allowing herself to be swept away by mere infatuation.

She considered Christy's playful nature—he seemed more captivated by fun and adventure than by the idea of settling down. Having grown up in a convent, she had always cherished a peaceful, steady life, a stark contrast to the thrill that seemed to follow him. Rushing into matters of the heart was not her style, especially when so much was at stake for her.

Thinking about David enveloped her in a warm glow. Being with him brought a sense of peace and happiness she rarely experienced around Christy. While Christy exuded lively energy, David's calm demeanor made her feel grounded and at ease. His comforting presence allowed her to forget the chaos of the outside world, giving her a sense of stability.

In contrast, Christy stirred romantic and alluring feelings within her, quickening her pulse but leaving her restless. She understood that such intense passions could fade with time, but what truly mattered was finding a companion who could provide lasting joy and serenity—a partner who could nurture her spirit.

David had dropped hints that he was paying special attention to her, yet she remained unsure of his true thoughts. The uncertainty kept her awake late into the night. Perhaps the award ceremony would bring some clarity, offering a chance to gauge David's feelings and where he truly stood. With these thoughts swirling in her mind, Liana drifted off to sleep, the promise of tomorrow whispering of new possibilities and the chance for deeper connections.

Chapter 12:
The Evening of Elegance

The award ceremony was organized by the government to honor the best companies in the country, and it was a prestigious event that drew media attention and photographers from far and wide. As Liana stepped into the grand hall, the atmosphere crackled with energy. Lavish chandeliers sparkled above, illuminating rows of elegantly dressed attendees, while the soft murmurs of anticipation reverberated throughout the space as guests settled into their seats.

This evening promised to be as much a celebration as an acknowledgment of excellence in IT. A distinguished crowd, adorned in formal attire, awaited the highlights of the night. Dancers and performers took to the stage, showcasing vibrant cultural displays, their rhythmic movements infusing the hall with energy and excitement, perfectly setting the festive mood for the evening ahead.

Liana, who found herself seated in the fourth row, could see the audience around her—executives, dignitaries, and innovators—all gathered to witness the achievements of their peers. Just before the ceremony began, David spotted her. Walking over with a warm smile, he greeted her, his eyes shining with a spark of appreciation.

"I'm so glad you could make it," he said, his tone genuinely welcoming as he took in her elegant appearance. "You look stunning, Liana." His gaze lingered a moment longer than usual, filled with admiration. "Let me show you to your seat. You'll have a perfect view from here." He gestured to her spot in the second row and made sure she was comfortably settled, then gave a brief nod before returning to his own duties with the VIPs seated nearby.

Liana watched him move gracefully through the crowd of high-profile guests, engaging effortlessly in conversations. His calm demeanor stood out in the lively atmosphere, and she admired how, even at such a young age, he navigated discussions with industry leaders and luminaries as if he truly belonged among them.

As the moment for the awards approached, a hush fell over the room when the announcer stepped onto the stage. Liana's heart raced with anticipation, excitement and pride bubbling within her as she awaited the announcement for "Best IT Company of 2024." When she heard David's company name being called, her excitement peaked.

"And the award for Best IT Company of 2024 goes to... Techno Bridge Solutions!"

The hall burst into applause, and Liana's excitement was nearly palpable as she watched David, looking polished in his tailored blazer and matching trousers, step up to the stage with unwavering confidence. He accepted the trophy with a proud smile, lifting it high for all to see. The cheers grew even louder, filling the hall as the audience celebrated his well-deserved success.

As the ceremony came to a close and guests began to mingle, Liana looked for David, eager to congratulate him in person. However, with the crowd shifting and everyone vying for his attention, he was nowhere to be found. Realizing he must be busy, she chose not to wait any longer and quietly slipped out of the venue.

The evening had been a whirlwind of emotions, and as she rode home in the taxi, the day's events settled within her, leaving her both exhilarated and exhausted. By the time she arrived home, dusk had given way to night. She changed out of her formal attire, still buzzing from the excitement of the night, and finally allowed herself to unwind. Feeling pleasantly fatigued, she lay down, letting her eyes close as she drifted into a peaceful sleep, warmed by the cherished memories of the evening.

Chapter 13:
A Surprising Evening

Thursday was always a whirlwind for Liana, especially after her Wednesday off, and today was no different. She didn't realize how late it was until she checked the clock—it was already 6:00 p.m., and she still had a few things left to wrap up. Around 6:30, she finally managed to leave the salon, grabbing a few groceries before heading home with plans to make a quick but satisfying dinner.

Once inside, she slipped out of her work clothes, changed into something comfortable, and prepared a savory fish stew, with fresh French bread on the side. After a quick shower, she hummed a tune, spritzed on her favorite mild cologne, and, feeling a bit relaxed, checked her phone. Just the usual messages, nothing unexpected. She sat down, ready to enjoy her meal while watching the news, when the doorbell rang.

Expecting her neighbor Doreen, she opened the door with a friendly smile, only to find David standing there, arms full of bags. "David! This is a surprise!" she exclaimed, her eyes widening as she took in the unexpected sight.

With a mischievous smile, he held out the bags and said, "Good evening, madam. May I come in?"

"Oh, of course," Liana said, stepping aside, barely able to contain her surprise. As he walked in, she couldn't help but notice his thoughtful grin.

"What's all this?" she asked, eyeing the bags curiously.

"These?" He laughed, setting them down. "Just a few essentials. I know how busy your Thursdays are, so I thought you might not have time to do any shopping."

Liana's heart warmed at the gesture. "David, that's incredibly thoughtful of you," she said softly.

David waved her gratitude away with a laugh. "Oh, don't think too much of it. But you owe me for disappearing on me last evening! I was looking for you everywhere after the ceremony, wanted to introduce you to my family."

Liana looked down, feeling a pang of guilt. "I'm so sorry, David. I was looking for you too, but you were so busy, and I didn't want to intrude. I thought I'd just congratulate you later."

He gave her a warm smile. "It's okay. I'll forgive you...on one condition."

"What's that?" she asked, raising an eyebrow.

He grinned, his tone playful. "Let me join you for dinner. I brought some pizza. Figured it'd be a perfect addition to whatever you've got cooking."

Liana laughed, shaking her head. "You think of everything, don't you? Well, you're in luck; I've made fish stew and got some fresh French bread."

"Perfect," David replied, following her to the kitchen. They set the table together, and soon it was spread with pizza, stew, bread, and a crisp salad. Their laughter and light-hearted conversation filled the room as they ate, each enjoying the easy, pleasant company of the other.

After they finished dinner, David helped her clear the table. Liana felt touched by his willingness to lend a hand, watching him move around her kitchen with the ease almost as if it were his own.

Afterward, she made them some hot coffee, and they settled down on the couch, their conversation drifting into more personal topics. David took a sip of his coffee and looked at her thoughtfully. "So, Liana, have you ever thought of opening your own salon?"

A small, wistful smile spread across her face. "It's always been a dream of mine," she admitted, "but it's not easy. I'd need a decent location, some money for equipment, and of course, I'd have to hire staff. It's a big investment, and I don't feel quite ready yet."

David nodded thoughtfully, setting his cup down. "Well, what if I could help with that?"

She looked at him in surprise. "What do you mean?"

"I mean, I'd be more than happy to invest in your salon. I could help you find a good location, and I know a few people who could help with setting everything up. You've got the talent, Liana—your salon could really take off."

The sincerity in his voice made her heart skip a beat. She could feel her walls softening, an undeniable warmth blooming in her chest. "David, that's...wow, that's a very generous offer," she replied, her voice barely above a whisper.

He smiled gently, his eyes meeting hers with an unwavering sincerity. "Liana, I believe in you. I've seen how dedicated you are to your work and how much your clients adore you. You deserve a place that's truly yours, a place where you can share your talent with even more people."

His words touched her deeply, and she could feel her usual cautiousness slipping away. She couldn't deny the depth of her feelings for David; his kindness, thoughtfulness, and belief in her dreams made her heart swell with gratitude and admiration.

"Thank you, David," she murmured, glancing down to hide the blush rising to her cheeks. "I'll really think about it."

He reached over, giving her hand a gentle squeeze. "Take all the time you need. I'll be here whenever you're ready."

They sat quietly for a moment, the unspoken connection lingering between them. As the evening stretched on, filled with shared stories and quiet laughter, Liana couldn't shake the feeling that, with David by her side, her dreams—both personal and professional—felt closer than ever before.

As David prepared to leave, he turned to Liana with a teasing grin. "You know," he said casually, "next Wednesday evening, I'll bring my mischievous little bundle along. I think you'd enjoy her antics."

Liana chuckled, warmth spreading through her at the thought. "Oh, that'd be wonderful! You're both welcome anytime," she replied, smiling as she walked him to the door.

"Good. Just be ready for some added chaos," he joked, giving her a wink before stepping out.

After he left, Liana paused at the doorway for a moment, his words resonating in her mind. She genuinely looked forward to seeing David, picturing the laughter and lightheartedness he would bring. It was a comforting thought—one she hadn't anticipated but found herself welcoming with open arms.

But then her thoughts shifted. Christy. He knew Wednesday was her off day too, and often took that as a cue to call or come by with spontaneous plans. He had a way of looking at her—those deep, mischievous brown eyes that made her feel like she was the only one in the room. She found herself yearning for that gaze, the way it left her both exhilarated and nervous all at once.

Yet, as her thoughts danced between David and Christy, a seriousness settled over her. This wasn't just a fleeting decision. Both men, in their own ways, were important to her, and it was becoming clear that they each wanted something more than friendship. Liana knew she couldn't let things remain casual—she had to make a choice.

She sighed, sinking into her couch. For so long, her life had been simple and free, no strings attached, no deep entanglements. But now... now it felt like her heart was being pulled in two directions. She wasn't sure if she was ready for such a change, yet here she was, faced with a decision she couldn't take lightly.

With a sense of resolve, she closed her eyes, allowing herself to drift into sleep, her mind still swirling with thoughts of David and Christy. As sleep finally took her, a quiet resolve began to form—no matter how long it took, she would make her choice with honesty and care, for herself and for them both.

Chapter 14:
A Bundle of Surprises and a Heartfelt Evening

The next morning, as sunlight filtered through her windows, Liana couldn't help but smile as she opened the parcels David had brought the night before. She began unpacking each item, astonished at how meticulously everything had been chosen. There were staples like rice and pasta, fresh vegetables, snacks, and even a box of her favorite herbal tea. Every item was carefully selected, as if he knew her shopping list by heart. Enough for a month, she thought, shaking her head in amazement. She chuckled to herself, "How on earth did he know I'd need all this?"

With a plan forming, she decided to subtly ask David about his intentions—carefully and diplomatically. She needed a clear answer, a hint at whether there was something deeper behind his thoughtful gestures. Christy still drifted in her thoughts, but she now felt it wiser to keep him at a distance until she had more certainty. Rushing wasn't her style, especially when it came to matters of the heart. This intriguing mystery with David deserved a bit more time to unfold.

Wednesday evening came, and just as promised, David arrived, holding the hand of a tiny, energetic girl with wide, curious eyes and a sweet smile that could melt anyone's heart. Rose, his sister's daughter, looked up at Liana with pure wonder, clutching tightly to David's hand as if she'd found herself in the middle of a fairytale.

Liana greeted them warmly. "And who is this adorable young lady?" She asked, bending down to meet Rose's gaze.

Rose blinked her big brown eyes and whispered shyly, "I'm Rose. Uncle David told me you're very nice."

Liana's heart melted on the spot. "Well, Rose, I think you and I are going to be great friends." She reached out her hand, and after a moment's hesitation, Rose let go of David's hand to hold Liana's, her tiny fingers wrapping around Liana's fingers like a little doll's grip.

As the evening unfolded, the room was alive with laughter and warmth. Little Rose seemed to have an endless supply of energy, darting around with wide eyes and giggles that filled the space. She'd pause now and then, catching sight of a new corner or knickknack and then scamper over to inspect it, her curiosity boundless.

"Aunt Liana!" Rose chirped, her face lighting up as she held up a small crystal figurine from the shelf. "What's this? It's so shiny!"

Liana knelt beside her, smiling. "That's a little glass unicorn, Rose. I've had it for a long time. Do you like it?"

Rose nodded enthusiastically, her little fingers tracing the unicorn's horn.

Rose nodded eagerly, her tiny fingers gently touching the unicorn's horn. "It's so shiny!" she whispered in awe, her eyes wide. "Is it magic?"

Liana smiled warmly, crouching down beside her. "Maybe it is, Rose. What do you think?"

Rose looked up at her, eyes sparkling with wonder. "I think... yes!" she said.

Rose's eyes sparkled at Liana's words, and with a burst of excitement, she began twirling around, arms spread wide like wings. "Look, Uncle David! I'm a unicorn!" she squealed, her laughter filling the room.

David clapped with delight. "I see a unicorn *and* a princess all in one! Luckiest guy in the room right here!" he said with a playful wink at Liana, making Rose giggle even more. Liana turned on the cassette player, filling the space with soft, cheerful music that seemed to lift everyone's spirits.

After a few more twirls, Rose ran over to David, tugging on his sleeve. "Uncle David, will you dance with me?"

He raised his hands in pretend hesitation. "Oh, I don't know if I can keep up with you, Rose! But maybe Aunt Liana can show us how it's done."

Liana laughed, extending her hand to Rose. "Alright, Miss Unicorn, are you ready to dance?"

Together, they swirled around the room, Liana guiding Rose as the little girl twirled and giggled. David watched them with a warm smile, his heart swelling as he took in the sight of Liana and Rose sharing this joyful moment.

After a little while, Liana knelt beside Rose, taking a moment to catch her breath. "You're such an amazing dancer, Rose! I think I'll need you to teach me some of your moves," she said, her eyes sparkling.

Liana brought over a tray with slices of cake, an assortment of snacks, and glasses of fresh apple juice, filling the room with sweet, inviting aromas. The treats seemed to cast a cozy warmth over the gathering, making the moment feel even more special. Rose's eyes widened with delight as she took a sip of the juice, her little face lighting up as she tasted the sweetness.

After a pause, Rose looked up at David with wide, hopeful eyes and a gentle smile. "Uncle David," she asked softly, "can I come back again soon?"

Liana's heart swelled at their sweet interaction. She leaned down and gently brushed Rose's hair away from her forehead. "Oh, I would love that, sweet girl. You're always welcome here!"

David looked at Liana, his gaze full of appreciation. "Thank you for making her feel so welcome. She's quite taken with you," he said softly, then added with a playful smile, "And, to be honest, so am I."

Rose had dozed off on the couch for a bit. "David," she said, keeping her tone light, "thanks so much for the things you brought that day. How did you know just what I needed?"

David smiled warmly, his eyes soft with a hint of amusement. "Well, I used to help my mom with all the shopping when I was younger," he replied. "So it's not exactly new to me. I picked up a few tricks."

She laughed softly, surprised but pleased with his answer, and decided to venture a little further. Taking a more playful tone, she asked,

"But why are you doing all this for me? You're making me feel like I'm getting some kind of...special treatment."

Without missing a beat, David stepped closer, gently taking her hand in his. His gaze was steady and warm, and his voice softened as he said, "Because I love you, Liana. I want to marry you soon. Think of this as our little 'rehearsal period,'" he added with a playful smile.

Liana felt her heart flutter, warmth rising in her cheeks. After a moment of letting his words sink in, she found herself asking, "Are you sure your family would agree with... this? With me?"

David's expression softened even further. "I have just one sister, and she'll be thrilled to meet you. My father passed away a few years back, and ever since, I've been the one holding things together. My family trusts my choices completely. They'll be supportive."

He smiled and, with a hint of teasing in his voice, added, "I was actually hoping to introduce you at the award ceremony. But when I looked around... someone had vanished."

Liana laughed and gave him a playful nudge. "Oh, really? If I'd known you had plans like that, I might have dressed for the occasion!"

David chuckled, glancing at her warmly. "Trust me, Liana—you're perfect just as you are."

They shared a warm laugh, their eyes meeting in a look of shared understanding and joy, as if they both knew this was just the beginning of something beautiful.

Liana glanced away, feeling a soft warmth rise in her cheeks. "It really has been a lovely evening," she murmured softly. "Thank you both for filling my home with such joy."

David leaned in with a playful spark in his eyes. "So, I guess you have plenty of secret admirer clientele at the salon?"

Liana chuckled, matching his tone. "Oh, a few of them are *very* concerned about my well-being," she said with a grin. "But I'm pretty sure it's mostly about keeping their favorite stylist around."

Liana raised an eyebrow, matching his playful tone. "And what about you, Mr. Chairman? With your position, you must have plenty of admirers."

David chuckled, his gaze softening. "I've had a few, I'll admit. But most were more interested in the title than in the person. Then someone with real charm came along... and, well, she's managed to reset my priorities completely."

Liana laughed, touched by the warmth in his words.

With a gentle smile, she responded, "Even if I do have secret admirers, I trust my instincts. I think I've already found the one I've been searching for."

He took her hand gently, his tone sincere. "Then let me keep bringing you happiness, Liana. I mean every word."

Liana's gaze dropped to their joined hands, her heart fluttering as she took in the depth of his words, feeling grateful for the man who seemed to know exactly how to make her feel cherished.

After lifting sleepy Rose onto his shoulder and gathering their things, David gently squeezed Liana's hand one last time. "I might have to bring Rose with me again—she won't let me come without her."

Liana smiled as she watched them leave, her heart feeling warm and full.

Once Liana had tidied up and had a quick meal, she washed up and settled onto her bed with her phone. She switched it to silent mode, careful not to let David catch her if Christy happened to call. She was always particular about these things. Glancing at the screen, she noticed she had five missed calls from Christy.

"Oh my God! Luckily, I put it on silent mode," she muttered, a bit frazzled. Before returning the call, she rehearsed what she would say in her head.

Taking a deep breath, she dialed Christy's number. "Hello?" came a slightly angry voice from the other end.

"What happened to you? Are you okay?" Christy continued, her concern flooding through the phone. "I was worried about your silence! Why didn't you answer the phone?"

"Hey, Christy, I'm here! Sorry about that. I had it on silent mode because I had some visitors today," Liana explained, trying to keep her tone light.

"Visitors? Who are they? Girls or boys?" Christy pressed eagerly.

"Um, no convent crowd," Liana replied, laughing a little. "Just some old friends. They came to see me after a long time. We had a nice time."

"Have they left now?" Christy asked, her curiosity piqued.

"Yeah, they just left," Liana confirmed. "But by the way, why did you call?"

"I had a plan to take you to a beach show! But since you didn't respond, I gave it up," Christy said, sounding a bit disappointed.

"Where are you now?" Liana asked, shifting a bit on her bed.

"I'm with some friends, just casual chit-chat at a restaurant," Christy replied, her voice relaxing.

"Okay, sorry for disappointing you. Have a nice time!" Liana said, hoping to wrap up the conversation without any more questions.

"Goodnight!" Christy chirped before hanging up.

As Liana placed her phone down, thoughts about the conversation lingered in her mind. "I must have accurately read Christy's playful side," she pondered, shaking her head lightly. Her thoughts then drifted to David. "David is simply irresistible; he exudes a comforting, fatherly warmth. But Christy? He seems far more focused on fun and games than on settling down."

"I need to be more cautious with Christy in the future," Liana realized, feeling an increase of affection for David alongside a hint of frustration with Christy.

Chapter 15
Heart's Dilemma

The next morning, Liana headed to the salon after a quick breakfast, her heart filled with warmth and a sense of good fortune. As thoughts of starting her own salon and the prospect of marriage swirled in her mind, she felt a mix of excitement and apprehension. However, she soon realized that she lacked trustworthy friends to share her aspirations with. The salon girls, though friendly, were often caught up in jealousy and competition, making it difficult for her to open up.

Her biggest dilemma was Christy. Ignoring him wouldn't be easy; their friendship was marked by unforgettable moments. Yet, she hadn't given him any assurances about her feelings or intentions, leaving her in a state of uncertainty. This weighed heavily on her mind, prompting her to consider confiding in her mother superior, the one person she believed could offer the guidance she desperately needed.

After a long day at the salon, Liana returned home and settled onto her bed, her mind racing. With a deep breath, she picked up her phone, feeling a mix of nerves and relief at the thought of speaking with someone who understood her. She had always respected her mother superior, who had often encouraged her to reach out whenever she faced challenges.

Dialing the number, she listened to the rings, anticipation building until she heard her mother superior's warm voice on the line. "Madam, it's me, Liana."

"Hi, Liana! I was just thinking about you. It's been a while since we last spoke. How are things on your end? Any problems?"

"Yes, Madam. I do have an issue, and it's rather sensitive. I know you're the only person I can turn to for advice," Liana replied, her voice steady yet filled with apprehension. She took a deep breath and elaborated on her complicated feelings about both Christy and David, explaining how their differing personalities affected her.

After listening intently, her mother superior offered her wisdom. "Liana, my dear, it's important to recognize the feelings you have for David and the potential for a brighter future with him. Christy, while he may hold a place in your heart, seems to be more drawn to playful pursuits rather than a serious commitment. This disparity is crucial to your happiness. It's clear to me that your heart resonates with David's dependable nature."

"But how do I separate from Christy without hurting him?" Liana asked, her voice tinged with worry.

"You must approach this with compassion and honesty," her mother superior advised gently. "Consider having a heartfelt conversation with Christy. Let him know that you value the friendship, but you need to prioritize your own path and well-being. It's crucial to be firm yet kind, ensuring he understands your intentions without leaving room for false hope. Remember, Liana, true friends will ultimately respect your decisions, even if they're difficult. You have the strength to navigate this, and by being true to yourself, you pave the way for your future happiness."

Liana felt a sense of relief wash over her as her mother superior spoke, her words resonating deeply within her. "Thank you, Madam. Your guidance means the world to me," she replied sincerely, feeling more empowered to face the challenges ahead.

"Of course, my dear. Always remember, you are not alone. Reach out whenever you need to, and trust your instincts. I believe in you," her mother superior reassured her.

After hanging up, Liana lay back on her bed, contemplating her mother superior's advice. She felt a renewed sense of clarity and purpose, ready to take the steps necessary to embrace her future and address her feelings with both Christy and David.

Chapter 16:
The Weight of Goodbye

That following night, Liana picked up her phone, her heart racing as she dialed Christy. His surprised voice came through the line: "Hi, Angel! What a surprise! I usually call you," he teased, laughing heartily. "I'm betting it's going to rain today since you called me—ha!"

"So, so! What's up?" Christy's enthusiastic voice crackled through the receiver, instantly lifting her spirits.

"Um, Christy, I'd like to chat with you tomorrow evening at our usual coffee shop. Can you make it around 7 PM?" Liana suggested, a knot of anxiety tightening in her stomach.

"Oh... tomorrow at 7 PM..." There was a brief pause on the other end. "I'm sorry, Liana, but I have an important appointment at 7:30 PM. How about we meet a little earlier, around 5 PM?" Christy proposed.

"Sure, I can make that work," she agreed, feeling relieved.

"Great! But you didn't say why the sudden meeting?" he pressed, his curiosity evident.

"Nothing much... just wanted to talk," she replied, trying to buy herself a bit more time. "Let's chat tomorrow. Have a great evening... Bye for now." With that, she ended the call.

The next day, as Liana prepared for their meeting, she felt a nervous flutter in her stomach. What if he didn't take it well? She needed to tell him she wanted to stop their friendship before it deepened. **But how do I say it?** She thought. **If he's as broad-minded as I hope, he'll understand. Surely he won't take this too hard.**

When she arrived at the coffee shop, the familiar aroma of brewing coffee mingled with the sweet scent of pastries. Liana took a deep breath, trying to calm her racing heart as she spotted Christy already seated, his face lighting up when he saw her.

"Hey there!" he exclaimed, standing up to greet her. "You're looking lovely as always."

"Thanks, Christy," she said, managing a smile as they settled into their seats. His cheerful demeanor lit up the cozy ambiance of the café, and Liana found herself trying hard to resist the pull of his captivating gaze. She understood that if she allowed herself to get lost in her feelings, it would be even harder to share what she needed to say.

After a few moments of light conversation, Liana felt the weight of the moment pressing down on her. "Christy, I genuinely value our friendship," she began, selecting her words with care. "But I need to be honest with you. I think it's best if we put a stop to this friendship before it deepens any further."

His smile slipped, and Liana noticed the color fade from his cheeks. "What? Liana, why? Did I do something wrong or behave badly?" he questioned, his voice a mix of confusion and concern.

"No, it's nothing like that," she said, her heart heavy as she saw his cheerful demeanor fade. "I just believe it's for the best. I need to concentrate on building my life with the person I've chosen to marry."

Christy leaned back in his chair, his expression serious. "So, who is the lucky guy who stole your heart?" he asked, a hint of hurt lacing his tone.

Liana bit her lip, hesitant to share too much, knowing how curious Christy could be and how much it might hurt him to hear everything. "Well, let's just say I might invite you to our wedding one day," she said with a playful smile, hoping to lift the heaviness in the air.

He chuckled softly, but Liana could see the pain reflected in his eyes. "You know, I didn't expect you to respond this way, especially since I sensed that you had a soft spot for me too," he confessed, his gaze dropping to the table. "Honestly, I've thought about marriage— with you, actually." He paused, taking a breath. "I've met other girls and had my share of flings, but I don't want to lie to you. After meeting you, everything changed. I know it'll take time for me to move on, but I'm determined to face this challenge."

A heavy silence fell between them, and Liana was overwhelmed by a bittersweet mix of sadness and relief. As they concluded their meeting, he drove her back to her apartment, the quiet stretching out like an unspoken farewell, each mile deepening the tension between them.

When they finally reached her doorstep, the car's engine hummed softly, but inside, a storm of emotions brewed. Liana turned to Christy, her heart pounding. "Well, here we are," she said, her voice barely above a whisper.

"Yeah..." Christy replied, his tone flat as he shifted in his seat, avoiding her gaze. "I guess this is it, then."

Liana felt tears prick her eyes as she searched for the right words. "Christy, I—"

"I just don't understand," he interrupted, his voice tinged with a mix of confusion and hurt. "I thought we had something special. I thought we were... moving somewhere."

She swallowed hard, battling her own emotions. "We did have something special. And I cherish every moment we spent together. You've been an incredible friend, but I need to focus on my future now. I'm getting married, and I can't keep pretending that this friendship can continue."

Christy's expression darkened, and he clenched his jaw. "So, that's it? Just like that, you're throwing everything away?" His voice trembled slightly, betraying the hurt beneath his bravado. "I thought you felt the same way about me."

"I care about you more than you realize," she said, her voice shaking as she fought back tears. "But I have to be honest with myself—and with you. It wouldn't be right for me to keep going like this. You deserve someone who can give you their whole heart."

"Liana..." he said, his voice softening as he looked into her eyes, the pain evident in his gaze. "You're the one I've wanted to build a future with. I thought... I thought I was the one for you."

"I'm so sorry, Christy," she said, tears spilling down her cheeks. "I never wanted to hurt you. You've been amazing, and I will always treasure our time together."

He leaned back, his shoulders heavy with resignation. "I guess... maybe I should've seen this coming," he murmured, a trace of hurt slipping into his voice. "I started hoping, especially after all those times we talked and shared moments together." His voice softened, barely a whisper, as he added, "It's just... hard to let go of someone who's come to mean so much."

"I know it is," she replied, her heart aching at his words. "And please know, a part of you will stay with me, always." She paused, her voice barely steady. "Just promise me... promise you'll find someone who can give you everything you deserve, someone who can make you truly happy."

He nodded slowly, his eyes glistening with unshed tears. "I'll try. But it'll take time. I never thought saying goodbye would hurt this much."

Liana stepped out of the car, her heart heavy with sorrow. "Goodbye, Christy. Please take care of yourself," she said, forcing a smile through her tears.

"Goodbye, Liana," he replied softly, watching her as she walked to her door, each step feeling like a fracture in her heart. As she turned the key in the lock, she took one last look at him, knowing this was the end of something beautiful yet painfully inevitable. "Goodbye, Liana," he said, his voice heavy with emotion.

With a deep sigh, she replied, "Goodbye, Christy."

As she closed the door, tears welled in her eyes. It was hard to let go, but sometimes, letting go was the only way to move forward.

Chapter 17:
New Beginnings, Old Faces

Liana could hardly believe the moment had arrived. After months of dedication, careful planning, and the constant support and guidance of her fiancé, David, she now stood proudly before her very own salon, *Liana's Haven*. Nestled on a bustling city corner, the salon exuded warmth and charm, drawing in passersby with its soft, inviting lights and stylish decor. It was everything she'd dreamed of—a cozy, welcoming space that already felt like a second home.

David gave her a reassuring nod as they stood outside, ready to cut the ribbon. He had been her unwavering support through every step of the journey. Madam Jean, her former boss, had also been an invaluable mentor, offering guidance and encouragement. Edward had enlisted his IT company's team to set up the salon's booking system and modern tech features, ensuring a seamless experience that would attract clients and keep them coming back.

Inside, a cozy gathering of friends and guests buzzed with excitement. Madam Jean, Liana's former boss, stood among them, along with familiar faces from the old salon. She had been both proud and a bit wistful when Liana shared her plans to move on. As a heartfelt farewell, Madam Jean had organized a send-off party, complete with touching speeches, laughter, and a few misty-eyed moments. The memory of that evening filled Liana with warmth, knowing she was supported by those who believed in her dreams.

When it was time for the ribbon-cutting, Madam Jean stepped forward, her voice full of pride. "Liana, watching you grow into such an inspiring young woman has been one of my greatest joys. I know you'll bring so much beauty, talent, and kindness into this space."

Liana blinked back tears as she hugged her former boss. "Thank you, Madam Jean. I couldn't have done this without you."

The ceremony went off perfectly, and soon, *Liana's Haven* was bustling with guests. Liana was training a few fresh faces herself, instilling her philosophy of going the extra mile for every client. It wasn't long before clients from Madam Jean's salon started trickling over, spreading word about Liana's incredible skills and the atmosphere she created.

One afternoon, just as she was finishing up with a client, she heard a familiar voice at the reception. Her heart skipped a beat, and she turned instinctively. There, standing by the counter, was Christy—with his arm around a beautiful, smiling woman. They hadn't noticed her yet, and she felt an unexpected pang of jealousy at how comfortable and intimate they looked together.

Trying to collect herself, she straightened her apron and approached the reception, putting on her warmest smile. "Christy!" she greeted, hoping her voice sounded natural.

He turned, surprised. "Liana! Wow, it's been ages," he exclaimed, his eyes brightening, though a flicker of unspoken emotions lingered beneath the surface. "When I saw *Liana's Haven*, I didn't realize it was your salon. That's amazing! Congratulations!"

Liana laughed softly, brushing off the sudden wave of emotions. "Thank you. It's been a lot of hard work, but worth every moment."

Christy smiled, though she noticed his gaze falter briefly as if recalling something. "Oh, Liana, this is Tina—my fiancée." He gently pulled the woman beside him closer. "She's looking for a haircut and a facial, and I thought I'd bring her to the best in the city."

Liana's heart clenched, but she kept her composure, extending a hand to Tina. "It's lovely to meet you, Tina. You're in good hands, I promise."

Tina smiled warmly, unaware of the brief, silent exchange between Christy and Liana. "Thank you! I've heard such amazing things about this place."

"Let's get started then," Liana said, guiding Tina toward a styling chair. She could feel Christy's eyes on her as she prepared Tina for her haircut, and her mind raced with memories, emotions, and a thousand things left unsaid.

As she worked, Christy leaned against the counter, watching quietly. She felt his gaze and decided to break the silence.

"So," she said, smiling at Tina through the mirror, "how did you two meet?"

Tina grinned, glancing at Christy. "Oh, it's a bit of a whirlwind! We met at a friend's wedding, actually."

Christy chuckled, though his eyes stayed on Liana. "It was one of those things, you know? Right time, right place."

Liana nodded, a smile never leaving her face. "Must be nice," she said softly, focusing on her work.

Once the haircut was finished, Liana guided Tina to the facial room, instructing the aesthetician who would be taking care of her. Christy remained outside, and Liana couldn't shake the feeling of tension between them—a conversation they both had left unresolved, hanging in the air like an unspoken promise.

Hope you're married by now," Christy said, his gaze locking onto hers.

"No, not yet. We're planning to tie the knot by the end of the month," she replied, a touch of excitement creeping into her voice. "Edward is currently busy overseeing the construction of our new house. I think we'll have everything finished before the month's end."

"Edward... that name sounds familiar. What's his surname?" Christy asked, his curiosity piqued.

Liana smoothly sidestepped Christy's question with a clever, lighthearted response. A quick twinge of regret flickered inside her—she'd said more than she intended. But she flashed a playful smile, keeping her tone breezy. "Oh, come on, that's nothing for you to dwell on," she replied, aiming for an easy, casual vibe to conceal her rapid heartbeat.

Christy paused, his brow slightly furrowed. "I'm just curious. I have a friend named Edward who's the Managing Director of an IT company called Techno Bridge Solutions. I've met him a few times while working on an advertisement for his company."

At the mention of Edward, Liana felt a flutter in her stomach, but she quickly steadied herself, resolved to keep her emotions under control. Just as the conversation seemed poised to delve deeper, Tina stepped out of the treatment room, glowing and full of joy. "Thank you so much, Liana! I feel amazing!" Liana couldn't help but smile back, genuinely happy for her. "It was my pleasure!"

Christy returned her smile, though a hint of sadness lingered in his eyes. "Take care, Liana."

"Take care, Christy."

As the door clicked shut behind them, Liana was hit with the familiar heaviness of farewell—one she realized she hadn't truly prepared for.

After coming to pick up Liana, David parked outside the salon, turned on some soft music, and leaned back, letting the gentle melodies ease the day's stress. About fifteen minutes later, Liana emerged, locked up, and slid into the passenger seat.

"Hi, sweetheart. How was the day?" he asked, smiling warmly.

"Not bad, Dave," she replied, fastening her seat belt. "How about you?"

"I had some important meetings today—outcomes were pretty good," he said with a satisfied smile. Liana beamed back, "That's fantastic! I knew you'd do great. Keep up the amazing work!" After a brief pause, she added casually, "Oh, by the way, Dave... do you know someone named Christy?"

David's eyebrows rose as he turned to her. "Christy? That name rings a bell... Oh, you mean the advertising guy?"

"Yes, that's him," she nodded with a slight smile.

"Ah, right! He did some brilliant work on an ad campaign for my company. Great guy—really knows his stuff and is fully dedicated to his work."

Well, I actually invited him to our award ceremony, David said with a nod of approval, but he mentioned he'd be out of the country on a business trip. David glanced at her, his curiosity piqued. So, how do you know him?

Liana hesitated briefly, then smiled. Oh, he used to be one of my regular clients at the old salon, she explained. Today, he came in with his fiancée for a haircut, and when he heard your name, he mentioned he knew you.

David chuckled, settling back in his seat. Small world, huh? Looks like he's a friend of both of us then. He thought for a moment, then added, we should invite him to the wedding. Sounds like it'd be nice to catch up.

Liana nodded, appreciating David's openness. "Yes, I think that'd be good."

With that, they fell into a comfortable silence, each quietly reflecting on the unexpected connections life could bring. The car hummed softly as they drove toward the evening, sharing a sense of anticipation for the future they were building together.

"Oh, by the way, Li, I'll need your guest list soon," David added. "I want to get the names printed on the invites as soon as possible."

"I'll finish it tomorrow. I'm almost done," she promised.

Later that evening, after dinner at her apartment, David settled onto the couch, resting his head in her lap as she gently brushed his hair. He closed his eyes, enjoying the moment of peace between them.

As they sat together, David looked up at her, a playful glint in his eye. "You know, Li, you're the one who's going to do my haircut before the wedding, right?"

Liana grinned and ran her fingers through his hair, teasingly fluffing it up. "Oh, absolutely! You think I'd let anyone else tamper with my masterpiece?" she teased. "Besides, I have big plans for your hair. I might just give you a daring new look... maybe a buzz cut? Or, how about some spiky highlights?"

David burst out laughing, covering her hands with his to stop her from messing with his hair. "No way! I trust you, but not *that* much! Promise me you won't make me look like a rock star reject."

She leaned down, smirking. "Hmm, we'll see. Just don't make me angry, or I might decide to surprise you with a bold new style. You'll be the most memorable groom in history!"

He chuckled, shaking his head. "You know, I'd rather have you cut my hair than anyone else... but please, keep the crazy ideas at bay. I'll need to recognize myself in the mirror."

"Alright, alright, no crazy styles... just a touch of perfection," she replied, planting a quick kiss on his forehead.

They both laughed, savoring the lighthearted moment, knowing there'd be many more to come.

Chapter 18:
The Choice of a Lifetime

Their beautiful day finally arrived, beginning with a grand and heartfelt church mass that seemed to wrap everyone in warmth and grace. Sunlight streamed through the stained-glass windows, casting a radiant kaleidoscope of colors over the guests, who sat with expressions of joy and anticipation, sharing in the love that filled the air.

As the procession began, Liana walked gracefully down the aisle on her uncle's arm, her gown flowing elegantly with each step. Just ahead of her, two adorable flower girls—little Rose and one of her friends from Montessori—scattered petals with shy smiles, while David's sister, Rose's mother, tried her best to keep the enthusiastic little ones calm and composed for this cherished moment. Following them were Liana's salon friends, dressed as bridesmaids, who added a touch of sophistication and warmth with their proud smiles, while David's cousins served as his best men, standing tall with pride for him.

Together, they painted a picture of love and unity, each detail adding a touch of magic to the day, making it feel like a timeless moment captured from a storybook.

As the mass came to a close, Mother Superior and the other convent sisters stepped forward to extend their blessings, their faces aglow with warmth and pride. Mother Superior, especially, shone with admiration. "Liana, you haven't just created a wonderful life for yourself; you've also chosen an exceptional partner to share this journey with," she said, her voice imbued with genuine warmth. Laughter flowed easily as they exchanged lighthearted, tasteful church jokes, infusing the air with a joyful spirit that uplifted the hearts of everyone present.

After a flurry of hugs, wishes, and joyful laughter, they headed to the Grand Orient Hotel, where the festivities would continue. Liana looked every bit like an angel as she entered the reception. Her gown shimmered, its delicate lace and flowing fabric creating an ethereal beauty that left everyone in awe. Her hair, perfectly styled by her salon team, framed her radiant smile. Beside her, David looked the epitome of refinement, his tailored suit and confident presence making them a striking couple.

The hotel was elegantly adorned, with flowers and twinkling lights creating a warm and inviting ambiance. It felt as if a fairytale celebration was unfolding, one that would be etched in everyone's memory for years to come.

As Liana and David entered the reception hall, they were met by Madam Jean and Doreen, Liana's vivacious neighbor, both approaching with beaming smiles. Madam Jean practically radiated pride, her eyes sparkling as she regarded Liana. "Well, Liana, you've finally made it!" she teased, lifting her glass in a toast. Liana embraced her warmly, planting a kiss on her cheek, while Doreen, with a broad grin, added, "I'll miss you, Liana, but I'm so glad to see you succeed."

With the toasts and playful jokes from David's friends, the couple's hearts felt full as they soaked up the love and laughter surrounding them. David's mother beamed with pride, her eyes glistening with joy as she raised her glass, offering heartfelt wishes for the newlyweds. His sister, Mary chimed in with a playful anecdote, her husband Leo chuckling beside her as they reminisced about their childhood antics. Little Rose, in her adorable dress, twirled around the couple, her infectious giggles adding to the warmth of the celebration. The family's presence created a cozy atmosphere, making the moment even more special as they all celebrated the bonds of love and togetherness.

After the clinking of glasses and laughter began to fade, David and Liana finally found a quiet moment together, and David turned to her, his eyes filled with admiration. "You look like a dream," he murmured, lifting her hand gently to his lips.

She smiled back, her heart brimming with happiness, and in that moment, words weren't necessary.

Just then, Liana noticed a familiar figure approaching—the unmistakable figure of Christy, looking sharp in a dark suit, his smile warm yet tinged with nostalgia. "Congratulations, Liana, David. You two look perfect together," he said, his voice sincere. Liana couldn't ignore the hint of something unspoken in his words, yet she felt a peace within her heart.

"Thank you, Christy. It means so much to have you here," she replied, meeting his gaze, before David extended his hand with a friendly nod.

"How about a photo with the three of us?" Christy suggested, his tone light and playful. David nodded readily, a smile on his face. "Of course! I'd be happy to include you, Christy."

As the photographer positioned them for the photo—Liana in the center, her husband on one side and her former crush on the other—she couldn't help but smile at the irony of the moment.

The universe certainly had a sarcastic way of reminding her of the past, placing her right between two chapters of her life. But now, as she looked at David, his hand warm in hers, she felt only strength and certainty. Whatever she'd once felt for Christy had faded into something friendly, a faint memory with no power over her heart.

In David, she had found the love she truly needed—a love rooted in trust, laughter, and a shared vision of the future. With a gentle squeeze of his hand, she closed the door on the past with quiet finality. This was her path now, her story, and she was right where she was meant to be.

True Partnership

A Love Rooted in Wisdom
Choosing a Lifetime Companion

In life, as in love, it's tempting to follow the pull of emotions without looking further down the road. Liana's story is a reminder to young readers: while feelings can be intense and consuming, they are often fleeting, like a gust of wind passing through. Real love, the kind that lasts a lifetime, is not just about excitement or chemistry—it's about companionship, trust, and shared goals.

It's easy to let the heart steer when emotions are high, but sometimes, our hearts can mislead us. Instead of rushing to follow every feeling, pause and consider whether the person beside you truly brings peace, joy, and stability to your life. A good partner will not only support you through the ups and downs but will also be a source of calm and strength when the world feels chaotic.

Choose a companion with whom you can build a future. Look for someone who listens, who respects you, and who is ready to journey with you through all that life brings. Use your wisdom, and take your time. A decision made with patience and insight will lead to a love that endures, supporting you not just today but for all your days ahead.

******************THE END*****************